ROAD RAGE

EMMA BRAY

CHAPTER 1

Bailey

"OH SHIT, OH SHIT, OH SHIT!" I chant under my breath as I struggle for control of the beast of a car under my fingertips.

Why in the hell I thought I could just jump right into an old stick shift convertible and drive it is beyond me. But in my defense, they make it look so easy on TV, and I was just so overjoyed to finally have a vehicle to get me to work that I didn't really stop to think about the logistics of everything—like how I barely passed the test to get my driver's license, have never even owned a vehicle of my own before, and have certainly never driven a stick shift before.

I know my uncle meant well when he left me this vehicle, knowing that I didn't have one, but right now, I'm wishing he'd left it to anyone but me.

I'm barely eighteen, but I've been on my own for a couple of years now. My uncle and I weren't particularly close, though he was always kind to me when he saw me, and he certainly didn't know that I'd ditched my last foster home and started living on my own.

I've been waitressing at this old dive down by the docks for a couple of years now, and I still managed to graduate high school while doing it. Being in school and working kept me off the streets during the daytime, and I was able to pick up meals and a bed at the homeless shelter for teens at night. Once I turned eighteen, I was finally able to take some of the money I'd religiously saved up and get my own place.

And I'm damn proud of it too. It feels so good to have a place all my own.

But I won't have the place long if I don't get to work on time because of this blasted car.

"Shit!" I scream again as I grip the wheel tightly and make a quick right turn so I don't miss the street leading to the docks.

A long, deafening honk blares out from the car I cut off, and I visibly wince as I glance in my rear-view mirror at the pristine-looking Audi I barely avoided hitting.

"Sorry, buddy," I apologize out loud to the random stranger, even though he can't hear me.

Actually, the driver could be a woman. I don't really know because the windows are tinted so dark I can't see in the vehicle at all, though something about the stark black vehicle has me immediately assuming it's a guy driving it.

I don't have time to pay attention to that, though, because I turn my eyes back to the road and say a silent prayer that I make it to work still in one piece.

The wind is whipping through my hair, and this would be such a perfect moment were I not terrified out of my mind because I suddenly realize that I just cannot freaking drive worth a crap.

I've always heard about those ditzy girls who just can't drive worth a shit, but I never imagined I'd be one of them. When I barely passed my driver's test by the skin of my teeth, I chalked it up to nerves.

But nope. I just can't freaking drive. And this right here proves it.

Period.

Cars are passing me left and right, honking at me. I'm sure I get flipped the finger more than once, and my cheeks are burning with humiliation.

Why can't this convertible's top stay up so I'm not on such blatant display? There might as well be a flashing neon sign hanging above my head that says, "Girl who can't drive."

I don't know much about cars. I don't even know what make or model this piece of junk is, but I do know that the top is messed up, hence why I'm maneuvering through traffic in the slightly chilly temperatures with the top down.

After several more near-miss accidents, I finally pull up to the joint I work at and jerkily put the car in park. Thank god there aren't any other cars parked on the street yet because yeah, good luck getting me to parallel park. I barely made it here in one piece as it is.

I don't know what I'll do when my shift is over and the car is sandwiched in with one in the front and back of it.

I'll probably just leave it sitting here. No way do I trust myself to get out of the parking space without jacking up a customer's vehicle.

I glance down at my phone and jump when I see the time.

Shit, the whole point of having a car and driving was to be able to get to work on time, but I'm going to be late if I don't haul ass inside right now.

I glance in the mirror to check my hair and grimace when I see my messy mane. I quickly twist it up into a messy bun and secure it with the elastic I keep on my wrist for emergencies just like this before I hop out of the car and hurry in to work.

I don't even bother locking it. What's the point when the top is down and it's all open inside? Besides, it's not like I have anything valuable inside to steal, and if someone is desperate enough to steal that clunker, hell they can have it.

Might even be doing me a favor.

———

Aidan

My irritation only increases when I watch the girl who cut me off in traffic step out of the old convertible that shouldn't even be allowed on the road. Not in the condition it's in anyway. It needs to be fixed up by a collector.

I don't know what possessed me to followed her. Actually, yes I do. Rage filled me at the disrespect of being cut off like she'd done, and nobody gets away with disrespecting me. No one.

If she was a man, I'd probably have already gutted her by now.

As it is, she's just this tiny little slip of a thing with wild locks of chocolate brown hair. I watch from my vantage point across the street as she twists it quickly up into a knot on the top of her head. Still, stubborn tendrils escape free to frame her heart-shaped face.

And it's not that I'm weak or anything, but I don't make a habit of harming women.

And, more importantly, the more I followed her and watched her nearly wreck into several other vehicles, the more my road rage began to fade when I realized that she hadn't cut me off as a sign of entitlement or disrespect.

The girl just can't fucking drive worth a shit. I wonder if she even has a license. If she does, whatever fucker gave it to her needs to have his certification revoked.

I drum my fingers on the steering wheel of my Audi as I continue to watch her, still irritated. She steps out of the vehicle, and I take in her faded, worn-out looking jeans and black T-shirt bearing the dive's logo.

So, she's a waitress here.

Figures.

I start to put my car into gear and pull off, but something stops me. I huff out a breath and pass a hand over my face in frustration.

If that girl gets back on the road, she's going to kill herself or others. And while I don't usually give a shit about people dying—hell, I'm one of the biggest contributors to the city's death toll myself, but in my defense, they're always scumbags who've got what they get coming to them—something about the thought of that girl crashing causes my chest to tighten.

So, I wait, glancing down at my watch every so often as the minutes tick by, watching the door to see when she comes out.

I'm just doing my civic duty, I tell myself. That's the only reason I'm stalking this girl like a psycho. Because she doesn't belong on the road, and I need to make sure of it she doesn't get back behind the wheel of that piece of junk.

I have so much other shit I should be doing. Running my empire. Making sure all the shipments have come in and gone out as they should have. Dealing with problems. Making sure fuckers stay in line. Sure, I've got guys on it who I know have it handled, but I don't keep my position as the city's most notorious crime boss by being an inactive figurehead.

No, I take a very hands-on approach to my reign.

But here I am unable to leave this spot without making sure one girl doesn't become a road hazard again.

I chuckle darkly to myself and shake my head as I pass my hand over my face again.

Apparently, I've finally lost my damn mind.

CHAPTER 2

Bailey

MY FEET ACHE from the threadbare shoes I've been wearing all night as I waited on customers. My cheeks ache too from the fake smile I had plastered all over my face when I really wanted to stab some of my rude, obnoxious customers with a fork.

My shoulders sag in relief when I walk outside after my shift and see that my car isn't blocked in.

I bite my lip as I contemplate the hunk of metal. I should be able to maneuver it out of the space and get it home. Surely, it's just like everything else. Practice makes perfect, right? The more I drive it, the more I'll get used to it, and the better I'll get at it.

I pull my keys out of the tattered bag I call a purse and start to walk over to the vehicle.

However, I yelp and jump when they're suddenly snatched out of my hand. My heart's racing as I turn to see a dark figure looming over me.

"Unbelievable," a deeply masculine voice smooth as velvet mutters.

I take a couple of steps backward and gulp as I take in the huge frame before me.

The man looks to be in his late twenties or early thirties. Tall and muscular, he towers over me. I'm a bit taken aback by the leather jacket he wears. It screams of money, so I have no clue what he's doing in this part of town. Most of the guys who frequent the dive wear dirty jeans and faded T-shirts.

A lock of dark hair falls forward over his forehead, and luminous green eyes glitter down at me. His mouth is pressed into a thin line, and something about him looks decidedly…dangerous.

Despite the expensive-looking clothing he's wearing, the man doesn't emit an aura of entitlement or refined gentleman.

Instead, he just emanates power. Pure, raw, masculine power.

He scowls when he sees me stepping backward, retreating from him. "Relax," he says, "I'm not going to hurt you."

I take another step back, and he huffs out an irritated sigh before saying, "I'm trying to keep you from hurting yourself."

"What?" I ask, shaking my head in confusion before I become indignant as I remember he snatched my keys from me. "Give me my keys back," I demand.

He barks out a laugh, though the sound is completely humorless. "Not a chance, dollface."

"You can't just take my keys!" My voice sounds as incredulous as I feel. Who the hell does this guy think he is? And what does he want?

He takes a step toward me and leans closer to my face, smiling ominously at me. "Oh, but I assure you I can, and I am. There's no way I'm letting you back in the driver's seat of a car—not after you nearly ran me off the road."

My heart pools at my feet as I look up at him in horror. Oh my god, the guy in the Audi! It has to be him.

I feel myself flushing with mortification. "Look, I'm sorry! I was trying to get to work on time, and I didn't do it on purpose. I totally didn't mean to cut you off like that, and I promise it won't happen again. Whatever you want, just please don't hurt me. I promise I didn't mean anything by it. It was a total accident…" I hate that I'm half pleading, terrified this psycho followed me to exact vengeance for some supposed slight. I swear to God if I ever get this piece of shit home, I'm never driving again.

He cuts off my blabbering with a raised hand. "Calm down. Again, I'm not going to hurt you," he scowls at having to repeat himself, and I can't help but notice how attractive he is even when he's frowning down at me.

Damn, I've got issues if I can find the man who essentially stalked me down over a road rage incident attractive.

"I just can't in good conscience let you back on the road. It's a miracle you made it here alive."

He's frowning down at me again, and I feel my cheeks burning with both indignation and humiliation.

Yeah, maybe I'm a shit driver, but who does this guy think he is forbidding me from driving like he's my father or something?

I snatch at my keys, but he pulls them out of reach.

It's my turn to scowl at him this time as I snap, "As touching as your concern is, it's none of your business, and I have to get home somehow."

"So, I'll drive you," he offers.

I stare up at him, surprised, and he looks just as surprised as I do at his offer.

"Um, no way," I scoff with my eyebrows raised. "How do I know you're not a serial killer or something?"

He actually looks amused. His mouth tips up at the corner, and his teeth gleam white in the streetlights as he answers, "If I wanted you dead, I'd let you drive this car again."

I stare at him, slightly offended, yet I can't deny the truth of his words. I'm a shitty driver. No point in denying it.

I shake my head. "I'll just catch the bus."

As if the universe is fucking with me, I hear the hiss of the bus as it passes by behind us. I see the man's eyes flick over my shoulder as he states stoically, "Last bus just left."

"I can just call a cab," I hedge, still too cautious, though my stomach drops at the thought of how much of my hard-earned wages will go toward the cab fare.

He sighs and passes a hand over his jaw as he looks up the street both ways before his eyes settle back on me. "Look, Bailey, I've told you two times I'm not going to hurt you. Just let me take you home so I know you get there safely."

I wonder how he knows my name, but then I realize I'm still wearing my name-tag pinned on my shirt. I continue to stare up at him, trying to gauge whether he has any nefarious, ulterior motives, but I honestly don't sense anything like that coming from him, and I like to think that I'm a good judge of character, living on my own as long as I have been.

Still, I can't help but tilt my head to the side as I ponder out loud, "Why do you care?" I really don't get it. Why this guy followed me after I nearly cut him off. Why he's now offering to drive me home so I don't kill myself. I mean, is he really that much of a good Samaritan? He certainly doesn't look it. If anything, he gives off dark angel vibes rather than guardian angel ones.

"Fuck if I know," he mutters before he puts a hand on the small of my back and begins leading me across the street to his car, obviously sensing that I've finally relented.

And against everything I was ever told about not accepting rides from strangers, I get into his car.

CHAPTER 3

Aidan

"WHAT'S YOUR NAME?" she asks me as I put the car into drive. She hasn't stopped staring at me like I'm a puzzle she's trying to work out ever since I expressed concern about her well-being.

If she figures me out, I hope she tells me what she finds because hell, I can't figure myself out today.

I don't know what it is about her that has me acting out of character.

I glance over at her, taking in her diminutive frame again. She's thin, and from the state of her clothing and shoes, I don't think it's by choice. I can recognize the signs of struggle and the streets from a mile away.

I was once there myself, after all.

The hair that escaped the messy knot on her head curls gently around her face, softening her features even more and only bringing out the gentle puff of her little pink lips.

Her eyes, though, are perhaps her most striking feature. A captivating hazel with flecks of brown, gold, and green in them. I find myself wanting to see them in better lighting, to stare into them and dissect all the colors within, find out which color is more predominant or if they just shift endlessly like the waves in the ocean.

"You know mine," she points out when I don't immediately answer her. "Seems only fair I should know yours too."

"Aidan," I answer her.

"Aidan," she repeats my name, and I feel a shiver go up my spine at the sound of it coming from her soft, slightly husky voice.

I shake my head. What in the hell is wrong with me?

"How often do you work there?" I ask her.

"Every night of the week," she says.

I frown. "What do you do during the day?"

She raises an eyebrow at me. "Are you mapping out my schedule or something?"

"Just answer the question," my voice comes out

rougher than I intend, but she doesn't argue.

She answers with a shrug, "I do odd jobs here and there, whatever work I can pick up from the temp agency or wherever."

I can read between the lines. This girl works her fingers to the bone for everything she has. She's surviving—not living.

Something about that bothers me.

I start to offer her a job, but I don't know what the hell I'd have her do. There's no way in hell I'm going to put her on stage as a dancer at one of the clubs I own, and I don't savvy the thought of her serving drinks in one my joints either. I frown just thinking of all the fuckers who'd be salivating over her.

She points out her turn up ahead, but there's no need.

I already know where she lives.

While I waited for her to get off her shift, I had my security run a check on her and send me all her details.

We drive the rest of the way in silence. When I pull up outside her building, I survey it with thinly veiled disgust.

The roof looks like it could crumble in at any moment, and the paint's old and chipped.

"Well, Aidan, um, thanks for the ride, and sorry again about cutting you off—"

I don't acknowledge her thanks. Instead, I bark out, "How do you plan on getting to work tomorrow?"

She pauses with her hand on the door. Her little brow furrows as she says, "I'll probably go back to taking the bus."

I can tell by the way she says it, she's not looking forward to the prospect, and who could blame her? The bus schedules are ridiculous. You have to leave two hours early just to go twenty minutes away, and they're always filled with the dregs of society.

I don't like the thought of her on a fucking bus.

She pauses uncertainly, as if she can sense she's not been dismissed.

I drum my fingers on the wheel before I hold my hand out, "Give me your phone."

She wrinkles up her little nose and looks at me with a haughty look in her eyes.

I roll my eyes in irritation and make an impatient gesture with my hand. "Come on, Bailey. Do I really look like I need to rob you? And if I was going to hurt you, I'd have done it by now."

She hesitates a moment before my words must finally make sense to her, and she hands over her phone without protest. It's a standard, old-school-style flip phone.

I program my number into it—my personal number

that only the highest members of my team have—before handing it back to her.

"I'll drive you wherever you need to go. Just contact me when you need to get somewhere."

She looks down at her phone and frowns. "That's not necessary—" she begins, but I cut her off.

"Just humor me, Bailey."

She bites her lips as she continues to stare down at her phone. Then, she looks back up at me with a question in her eyes. "What about my car?" she asks.

My lips twitch, though I don't know why. "Don't worry about it. I'll have it taken care of."

She opens her mouth like she's going to say more before she finally closes it and shakes her head like she doesn't know what to think of me. Join the club, sweetheart. I don't know what the fuck's going on either.

I watch as she gets out of my vehicle without another word.

She doesn't look back as she enters the building and goes up to her apartment. I watch the lights come on in her window. She's got the blinds drawn, so all I can see is her shadow moving through the blinds, and a feeling of pride wells up in me that she's not like one of those idiotic women who get undressed with their blinds open for all the city to see.

I don't know how long I sit there, contemplating the dark-haired beauty, but when I finally pull away from her building, the lights in her apartment have been long off.

———

Bailey

I walk outside the next morning and pause when I see the Audi sitting on the curb in front of my apartment.

He's already stepping out of the car by the time I reach the sidewalk.

"What are you doing here?" I ask him cautiously as it hits me all over again just how tall and powerful-looking this man is. He's wearing leather again and looking just as polished yet somehow dangerous as he did yesterday.

I can't help glancing down at my faded jeans and tee and worn-out shoes.

This man and I are worlds apart.

Or, are we? Though Aidan might look well put together, there's something raw about him too.

Like he knows the streets. Like maybe he's from them.

Or in charge of them, a little voice inside my head whispers.

"Something told me you wouldn't call me." He's frowning at my disobedience.

I raise my chin. "Look, I seriously don't need you to chauffeur me around everywhere. Thanks for yesterday, but I'll be fine taking the bus from now on."

As much as I hate taking the bus, I do have my pride, after all.

And apparently, this man doesn't give a shit about that because he rubs a hand over his mouth in an irritated gesture before he looks up at the sky as if he's praying for strength. When he finally pins his green gaze back on me, my breath catches at the command in both his eyes and his tone when he says, "Just get in the car."

However, I'm not one to be commanded. I bristle and continue walking down the sidewalk away from him. I've never let anyone order me around, and I'm not fixing to start now.

I hear something behind me that sounds like a half-laugh, half-growl, and then he's right beside me, grabbing my arm to spin me back around to face him.

I'm met with fiery green eyes and a frowning countenance. "I'm not used to having my requests ignored," he warns me.

I cock my head to the side and blink. "Was that a request? It sounded like an order, and I'm not used to taking orders." I frown back up at him. I don't care how big he is or how powerful. I'm not going to let him push me around.

He stares at me a moment like he doesn't know quite what to make of me before he finally gives an incredulous laugh and relents with, "Will you please stop being so stubborn and let me drive you to wherever you need to be?"

His voice trips over the *please*, giving me the impression that this isn't a man who's used to asking for anything—much less saying 'please.'

I continue to study him for a moment, once again wondering why he's taken such an interest in my welfare.

I can't stop myself from asking him either. "Again, why do you care? I'm nothing to you."

His jaw hardens—at what I said?

But then his eyes seem to soften as they pass over my face. "Will you just get in the car?" he asks me more softly this time, his voice almost pleading.

And for some reason, I do.

CHAPTER 4

Bailey

AND SO, it begins. This strange ritual of Aidan driving me everywhere I need to go.

I don't ask him again why he's so insistent on it, and he doesn't offer me any explanation.

I'd be lying if I said I'm not thankful for it. It makes getting around a lot easier.

But it's odd how he's made himself available to my beck and call like this. I don't understand why he's doing it.

What does he get out of this?

I still feel bad about texting him asking for rides,

but if I start off walking without texting him, he somehow just so happens to show up.

Like he's following me.

Something tells me that should bother me way more than it does.

But for some reason, it doesn't. I actually feel... somehow safer knowing that he always seems to know where I'm at.

Like for once in my life someone is really watching out for me.

It's still odd, though. He doesn't speak much. Aidan isn't the talkative type. When we do talk, it's always about me. He asks me how my work is, more about my past.

And I find myself babbling on, releasing my soul to him. Maybe it's because I've never really had anyone to talk to, and now that I do, I can't shut up.

But he always listens with seemingly rapt attention as he weaves expertly through traffic, driving so easily —in a way I never could.

He deflects all my questions about him back to me with vague half answers—if he even gives any answers at all.

I still don't have a clue what he does for work that allows him to have time to run an eighteen-year-old girl around everywhere. All I've been able to get out of him is, "I'm my own boss, so I can do what I want."

Yeah, that's very specific.

And he still wears the leather jacket every day. I don't know what he does in between driving me around, but he always looks the same. Stylish jeans, white tee shirt that hugs every muscle in his body, and leather jacket.

Maybe I shouldn't be letting him do this, but something tells me that I can't stop this man from doing anything he really wants to do, and for some reason, he has decided to drive me around everywhere.

Plus, who I am to argue when the universe has thrown me a bone? I'm tired of walking and public transportation.

Aidan's attention is actually…nice.

True to his word, he took care of my vehicle. He told me he had it in safekeeping in a garage for whenever I decided what I wanted to do with it.

The look on his face made it clear driving it isn't one of my options.

I suppose I should be offended that he has the audacity to ban me from driving, but I did almost run the guy off the road, so I guess I can't really blame him.

I don't want to drive anyway.

Especially if he's content to drive me around.

But how long is this going to last? Does he really plan on being my chauffeur until the end of time? I study his profile every day, trying to figure out what his end game is, but I'm no closer to figuring him out than I was on day one.

And I can't bring myself to ask him how long he plans on doing this.

Because I dread hearing the answer. I dread the day he comes to his senses and just stops. It's not that I'll miss the rides so much—though it definitely beats public transportation.

It's that I'll miss…him.

Him and all his moody, broody presence. Even his silence is more company than I'm used to.

Aidan is an enigma.

But somehow, I feel like he's *my* enigma now. I'm probably getting way too attached to this guy, but I can't help it.

Things in my life have just seemed to go better since he's been around too. My boss doesn't seem to yell at me nearly as much. In fact, he's being way nicer to me than he's ever been.

The customers aren't making the lewd comments they used to or hitting on me like they used to either.

I don't know if it's just coincidence or something to do with Aidan, but I'll take it because it makes my life easier.

"So, how was work?" he asks me as I get into his car after my shift.

He looks the same as always—darkly alluring in

that leather jacket and with his green eyes almost glowing at me in the darkness like a cat's or something.

"It was good," I tell him with a smile, feeling lighter than I have in a long time. "One of my coworkers actually invited me to a party tomorrow night."

I see him frown, and I rush to add, "I don't need you to take me there. You already do enough. I can just hitch a ride with Xavier." Xavier, one of the bartenders who works with us has already offered to pick me up and take me to the party. I usually never attend any parties with my coworkers, too busy trying to make money and used to sticking to myself, but things have been looking up for me ever since I almost ran Aidan on the road, so I thought, what the heck? I'll try to get outside my comfort zone and socialize with a few people.

"Xavier..." he repeats the name slowly, though something about the way he says the name with an undercurrent of a growl has me instantly on alert.

"He's one of the bartenders," I tell Aidan, glancing at him curiously, wondering why he's acting so weird.

"No," Aidan suddenly barks.

I jump back at his tone and blink at him. "What?" I ask in confusion.

"You're not going," Aidan's tone brooks no argument, and my brow furrows as I give a humorless laugh.

"No offense, but you can't tell me what to do, Aidan," I retort, getting more pissed by the second.

He doesn't even acknowledge what I said. Instead, he growls, "I forbid it."

I blink again, my hackles rising. "Forbid it?" I repeat like I didn't hear him correctly.

He does something then that he's never done before. It's so unexpected all I can do is stare at him in shock as he reaches across the console and grabs my hand in his, his grip firm. He turns his head to look directly at me as he states somberly, "It's not safe, Bailey."

All I can think about is how tiny my hand feels in his and the tingles that are running up my arm from where he's touching me, skin on skin.

All this time of him driving me around, he's never made a move to touch me. That's why I never even entertained the thought that he might be interested in me romantically—not that I'm entertaining it now.

But it's obvious at my body's reaction to him that I am insanely attracted to him. I mean, I've always noticed how hot he is, but I've done my best to ignore it, telling myself that's not what he wants from me.

And I still don't think he's interested in me that way. My cheeks burn when I remind myself how much wealthier than me is. I'm probably just some sort of charity project for him. Hell, I don't know.

I jerk my hand back from him as if scalded by his touch, and he instantly releases me. "Why isn't it safe?" I ask him. "It's just a party with some of my coworkers. I work with them every day. They're nice people."

His jaw hardens, and he looks back at the road. I see his knuckles whiten from where he's gripping the steering wheel so tightly. I don't know what his deal is, but he's confusing the hell out of me and frankly, staring to creep me out a bit.

He finally huffs out an irritated sigh. "Just trust me on this, Bailey. Don't go."

I stare at him, and he glances over at me, his green eyes flashing with irritation at his orders being questioned.

I don't say another word to him the rest of the drive to my apartment, and he, of course, makes no move to break the silence either.

When he finally puts the car in park outside my building, he opens his mouth like he might say more, but it's too late.

I hop out of the car and run into my building before he gets a chance to, more confused and irritated myself than ever.

Fucking Aidan.

CHAPTER 5

Aidan

I HAVE a feeling she's not going to fucking listen to me. So, here I am sitting down the street outside her apartment to make sure she doesn't try to sneak out to go to that damned party.

I'd like to slit the throat of whoever invited her.

She doesn't need to be going to parties.

Putting herself in danger.

My hands fist on the steering wheel as I think of one of my enemies getting ahold of her. Panic and rage begin to flood my chest, and I take deep breaths in through my nose in an attempt to calm myself.

Bailey has come to mean more to me than anyone in

this world ever has. I don't know what it is about her, but I crave her presence.

Even when I sit here in this car sullenly and don't speak hardly two words to her, she's content to sit quietly with me. If I ask her a question simply to hear her voice, she happily chatters on about the little mundane aspects of her day.

I listen with rapt attention, absorbing everything about her. I want to hear every thought in her pretty little head.

She fascinates me.

Her safety is paramount to me. It has been from the moment I first saw her. And I know I should have given her a driver by now, removed myself from this situation, but the thought of someone else spending all this time with her tightens my chest.

I want to be the one absorbing in her essence, learning everything about her—like the way she bites that puffy pink lip when she's worrying about something or the way she absently twirls a chocolate curl around her finger when she's deep in thought.

I could put one of my guys on watching her, staking out her house, knowing where she is at all times, but the truth is I get almost jealous with rage at the thought of someone else watching her like this.

She's mine. Mine to watch. Mine to protect.

It started off with me just giving her rides, but the more I'm around her, the more obsessed I become.

The more I find myself sitting outside wherever she's at, eyes constantly scanning the perimeter, looking for any threats.

The more I find myself threatening fuckers about her safety.

Like her piece of shit boss. My lip curls up into a sneer when I remember how the slimy fucker nearly pissed himself when I told him how things were going to be from now on. When Bailey got into my car damn near in tears over him yelling at her one day, I quickly put a stop to that.

I put the word out. Everywhere she goes now, people know whose protection she's under.

They wouldn't dare harm her because my reputation precedes me. They know how dire the consequences would be for messing with anything that's mine.

I only did it to protect her, knowing that my name carries a certain amount of clout in this city.

However, my name also carries a certain amount of notoriety, and by so publicly claiming her and having her be seen getting in and out of my car so much, I might have actually put her in even more danger.

My enemies know she's my weakness now. If they see an opportunity, they'll take her just to get to me.

My fists tighten on the steering wheel again. Damn it all to hell!

I hate myself for being so weak, for not thinking this all the way through when I threatened every fucker within a fifty-mile radius regarding her safety.

I contemplate—not for the first time—just taking her home with me and locking her up. She doesn't need that fucking waitressing job. I can give her everything she wants and more.

But fuck me, she's only eighteen. Barely fucking legal. I'm ten years older than her and way too dark for her light.

Not to mention the fact that she might really hate me if I just kidnap her.

Doesn't stop me from considering it.

But my hands are dirty. I'm not worthy to touch her.

No matter how much I might want to. No matter how hard my cock gets sitting beside her every day, smelling her sweet fragrance, imagining how soft her skin is.

I'm hard as a rock right now just thinking about her, and I'm not even imagining her naked.

Fuck, that's what she does to me.

Fucking damn it.

I feel precum leaking from my tip, and I know I won't be able to focus if I don't get a handle on myself.

After trying to make myself go down to no avail, I finally curse and grab a handkerchief from the glove department.

Yeah, I've had to take to keeping something in my car just for moments like this. Moments when I get so hard up for Bailey I can't think straight.

It doesn't even take me two minutes before I explode, jerking my fluids into the cloth. All I have to do is think of her cherry-ripe lips and imagine how they'd taste and I'm pumping.

It's really rather embarrassing how short I last when jacking off to just the image of my obsession's lips.

I stuff my dick back in my pants, the tension in me barely abated before it already begins to rise again.

Jacking off only takes the edge off. All I have to do is think of her again, and my damn cock is already rising for more, knowing that it was cheated of the real thing.

I continue my silent vigil outside her apartment. I'm starting to get hopeful that maybe my girl is going to listen to me.

But then my eyes damn near bug out of my head when her lithe little form waltzes out of the building wearing nothing but some little white dress that flutters around her thighs. It barely covers her. If the wind blows or she bends over one time, everyone is going to get a good look at her tight little ass.

She has on little red kitten heels, and my fists clench on the steering wheel again as I see nothing but red.

Her dark curls are flowing down to her waist, wild and untamed. She looks like a little lioness, and I can't help imaging what those curls would look like bouncing around her head as I thrust up into her, shaking her whole body.

I shake my head to get my focus back. I'm fucking furious. I want to ask her why the fuck she has clothing like this.

She looks tempting. Too fucking tempting. No man will be able to resist her like this, and I don't even want to think of what my enemies would do if they got ahold of her looking like this.

I watch as she glances around nervously, checking to see if I'm around, no doubt. The little minx knows she's being disobedient, and I'm so fucking mad that she would disobey me like this I can't fucking see straight.

Once she decides the coast is clear, she takes off walking down the street. Down the motherfucking street! She won't make it two blocks before someone tries to kidnap her ass.

I tighten my jaw so tight I'm surprised the fucker doesn't snap in half before I fling the door of my car open and begin stalking across the street over to her.

CHAPTER 6

Bailey

"OH, HELL NO," Aidan's voice suddenly growls from right behind me.

My heart damn near jumps out of my chest at his sudden appearance. I spin around to face him, a hand over the offending organ that's galloping away under my breast. "Aidan!" my voice comes out breathy. "Shit, you scared me."

His face is sterner than I've ever seen it, and the anger in his eyes shines through like a flash of lightning as he glares down at me. He's practically vibrating with rage. I can literally see his hands shaking, and I instinctively gulp and take a step back from him.

"This," he hisses as he steps toward me, making a motion with his hand over my body from head to toe, "this is not happening, dollface."

I instantly stiffen at his tone. "Yes, it is," I retort back at him firmly. "I told you I don't need you to drive me, but I *am* going to that party, Aidan. Xavier's going to pick me up a couple of blocks down the road." I was only going to have Xavier pick me up a couple of blocks away to avoid Aidan somehow finding out and causing a scene, but hell, he already found me slipping out, so what does it matter now?

He stares at me a full minute, his jaw ticking, before he smiles, but it's not a friendly smile. It's dark and causes a shiver to run up my spine. He laughs a wicked laugh before he tells me almost calmly with a nonchalant shrug, "That's fine. Get in the car with him, Bailey."

I stare at him suspiciously, already picking up on the fact that he's not really relenting but that he's being sarcastic.

"Give me something to do later," he adds ominously, and I hear the clear threat in his words.

My breath catches at his implication. Something about Aidan has always told me he dances to the beat of his own drum. I think I've always suspected that he toes the other side of the law, but I don't think it ever really resonated with me just how truly dangerous he could be until this moment.

"You can't stop me from going," I persist stubbornly, though why I don't really know. I don't really know the people at this party that well. If I'm being honest, I don't really care about going that much anyway. In fact, I started to chicken out and just stay home to begin with, but the thought of Aidan *forbidding* me from doing it only made me want to do it even more—out of spite. As immature as it may be.

He grins a truly evil grin then. "Try me," he dares.

I stare at him for a moment, trying to decide what to do, and then I turn on my heel and take off running down the sidewalk.

I don't know why I do it. I know there's no way I can ever outrun Aidan. His stride is twice the length of mine, and I know he's fit and strong.

It thunders ominously in the distance as I run as fast as I can in my heels. Blasted heels!

I don't even get half a block before I feel his strong arms wrap around me from behind, yanking me back against his granite chest.

Thunder sounds again, and then lightning cracks before a sudden torrent of rain dumps from the sky. It doesn't start off with any warning sprinkles. It's just an instant deluge, soaking me to the skin immediately.

Aidan spins me around in his arms, and I look up at

him, seeing the lightning reflected in his green orbs. His eyes are flashing down at me harder than the lightning as he takes in my drenched appearance.

He looks just as beautiful wet as he does dry, water droplets causing that lock of hair to fall over onto his forehead, beads of water rolling down his face, glistening on the wet leather of his jacket.

Whereas I'm sure I look like a pitiful, drowned kitten.

His gaze wracks over me where my white dress has become see-through and is clinging to every curve of my body.

My cheeks burn as I realize he can probably see the hard buds of my nipples poking through the fabric, my skin showing through the now nearly translucent dress.

His eyes darken. He whips his jacket off and wraps it around my shoulders before scooping me up into his arms effortlessly.

My arms instinctively go around his neck to hold on, and I can't help breathing his aroma in deeply. He smells like spice and citrus and rain all mixed together. He smells so good it's enough to make me dizzy.

"Infuriating fucking girl," he growls as he begins stalking us back to my apartment.

I don't protest when he carries me up the stairs to my floor and goes straight to my door without even having to ask me which apartment I'm in. Somehow, it makes sense that he just knows. Aidan seems to always know where I'm at.

He kicks my door in with one foot, muttering something about piece of shit apartments and getting me better locks.

He sets me down on the counter in my kitchen. My feet dangle several feet off the floor as I sit there, a dripping mess, looking up at him, still partly in shock at everything that's happened.

He carried me up four flights of stairs, but he's not even panting. He shakes he head like a big beast shaking water off its fur, and water goes flying everywhere.

His jacket slips off my shoulders, and I see his eyes flick down over my body again, darkening as they do so.

"Why are you so infuriating?" his voice comes out gravelly as he stares down at me.

I feel naked as his eyes drink me in, and I feel my nipples harden painfully. "I'm not—" I begin, but he interrupts me by slamming his lips down over mine in a fierce kiss.

Good god, the electricity that shoots through me the moment his lips touch mine.

His lips are wet, and heat rushes through me immediately at the contact. He doesn't waste any time and pushes his tongue into my mouth at my gasp as he grabs both sides of my face with his big hands.

He growls into my mouth as his tongue seeks out mine, swirling and dancing with it in an erotic tango that has me mewling and leaning into him.

My entire body suddenly feels like it's on fire despite the wetness of my thin clothing.

"So fucking sweet," he whispers against my lips as he pulls back. "Like I knew you would be."

I look up at him and see his green eyes blazing down at me with an intensity that takes my breath away. "I can't believe you thought I was going to let you parade around in this flimsy thing." He growls as he fingers the hem of my wet dress, his eyes flaring with lightning again.

"You can't tell me what to do—" I start to stubbornly retort, but he effectively silences me by kissing me again.

I melt into his kiss and forget why I'm protesting in the first place.

This time he doesn't stop at my lips. He begins to kiss down the side of my neck and over my collarbone until he reaches the swell of my breasts.

My nipples are so tight they hurt, and then he takes one in his mouth, sucking at it through the wet fabric of my dress.

And good lord.

I gasp, my arms flying out to wrap around his head. His hands steady me on the counter with a hand firmly planted on each side of my waist.

He licks and sucks at one nipple before moving to the other, and my god, I can't think of anything but how delicious the sensation is.

"Aidan," I moan his name, not sure what I'm asking for but knowing that I don't want him to stop.

"Yes, babydoll," he whispers as he moves his lips to my shoulder and begins licking and kissing his way from there down the sensitive inside of my arm. "Say my name."

Something hot unfurls inside me at the husky tone of his voice and the way his lips feel like fire branding my skin everywhere they touch.

He finally drops to his knees in front of me and pushes my wet dress up to reveal my white panties that are sticking to my skin, soaked through from both the rain and my body's own natural juices.

I flush when he just kneels there looking at me. I start to instinctively close my legs, but he holds them wide with a hand on my thighs and looks up at me, heat flaring in his dazzling green irises. "Don't hide that pretty little thing from me, Bailey."

I bite my lip as his eyes drop back down to the juncture between my thighs. The next thing I know he's leaning in and kissing me there, through the wet fabric of my panties, until he hooks a finger under them and rips them clean off me.

I gasp at both the motion and the sensation of air suddenly hitting my exposed private parts, but then his mouth is on my bare flesh, and my head falls back.

Oh my god, it feels so sinfully good. He's kissing me there like he kissed my mouth, open and with his tongue swirling over me. I feel his finger beginning to push into my hole, and I automatically tense up.

He makes a sshhing noise as he continues to move it gently out of me, pushing deeper each time, and then his whole body stills.

He stops kissing me and looks up to meet my eyes, shock written on his face. His finger is still held inside me, and I'm throbbing around it, feeling fuller than I ever thought I could.

"You're a virgin?" he asks me incredulously.

CHAPTER 7

Aidan

HER CHEEKS TURN PINK, and she bites her lip as she nods in embarrassment.

I can still feel my finger pressed against her hymen, and I pull it back, not wanting to break her barrier with anything but my cock.

Blood rushes to my already engorged cock so fast upon the confirmation that nobody else has had her that I almost get dizzy.

Mine. Mine. Mine.

Nobody else will ever touch her.

I don't know how the fuck she's made it to eighteen

without losing her virginity. She's gorgeous as hell, and I know all the boys must have been dying to get between her legs. My jaw hardens just at the thought of some fumbling boy taking her virginity, hurting her, not giving her the pleasure she deserves.

"Have you ever had an orgasm?" I ask her.

She flushes again before she shakes her head.

Holy hell. That knowledge unleashes something primal within me. Every cell in my body is screaming at me to claim her, breed her, make her mine in every way.

"I'm going to take care of you right now, baby," I tell her, making no effort to hide the lust in my voice. I don't think I could hide how much I want her even if I tried. "Is that okay with you?"

God, I want her beyond all thought or reason, but I have to make sure she wants this too.

She nods down at me shyly, and I raise an eyebrow at her, needing to hear her say it.

Her face colors even more as she realizes what I'm waiting for. "Yes," she finally breathes. "Please, Aidan."

That's all I need to hear, her little voice, half begging me to pleasure her.

My mouth is already salivating as I lower it to her pink flesh once again.

How does she taste like fresh cherries? She's so

sweet, it's a good thing I'm not diabetic or I'd go into a sugar coma.

And there's nothing like the rush I get when I feel her squirming and tensing beneath me as I swirl my tongue over her little clit while gently prodding her pussy with my finger. She's so tight and virginal, it's all I can do to get one finger in her.

But I have to ready her for my cock, so I slowly insert another finger, watching her face for her reaction as I continue to suck on the little pearl between her legs.

Her eyes are wide, and her mouth falls open in a silent gasp. She's panting. Her whole body is flushed. A light sheen of sweat is breaking out on her skin. Her wet hair is plastered against the side of her face, and I swear I've never seen a more beautiful sight.

I crook my fingers inside her, rubbing the spongy spot against the front wall of her pussy, and she screams, throwing her head back as I feel her begin to pulsate around my fingers, gripping and sucking them greedily as fluid gushes over my hand. A jet of precum shoots out of the tip of my cock, staining the inside of my boxers as I imagine her pussy pulsating around my dick like that. Fuck, I can't hold back much longer. I'm going to fully spill myself in my pants soon if I don't fuck her.

I continue licking her, savoring the creamy taste of

her release as she twitches in my arms until she goes lax.

I catch her back in my hands before she falls back onto the counter, rising to pull her against my chest, my arms supporting her slight weight.

I feel her body trembling and stroke her hair back out of her face, looking back into those hazel eyes that haunt my every waking and sleeping moment.

"I need you, Bailey," I tell her.

She wraps her arms around me and nuzzles her head into my neck, and I feel my chest squeeze painfully at the trusting gesture.

"Tell me you're mine," I order her gruffly.

"I'm yours," she breathes into my neck dreamily, but I'm still not satisfied.

I pull back and hold onto her upper arms to force her to look up at me. I want to make sure she knows what she's agreeing to, that she's not just fuckstruck after her first orgasm.

"Do you understand what I'm asking you?" I ask her almost desperately. "There's no going back. Once you're mine, you're mine." I don't know why I'm making a big deal out of this. Whether she knows it or not, this girl has been mine from the moment she damn near ran me off the road.

Maybe it's that I already know how badly I'm obsessed with her and that it's only going to get worse once I get inside her. I'm already paranoid about her safety as it is, and I know my protectiveness is only going to increase tenfold once I make her mine in every way—if it's even possible for me to become even more psycho over her.

"No parties with other guys," my face darkens at just the thought. "No flimsy fucking dresses that become see-through in the motherfucking rain." I jerk the sodden excuse for clothing off her body, leaving her totally bared before more. "You have to do what I tell you, and not because I'm trying to control you but because I'm trying to protect you."

"Is that why you insisted on driving me around everywhere?" she asks me innocently. "To protect me?"

I let out a shaky laugh, "That and you got under my skin in a way no one else ever has. Plus, it was obvious you're a hazard to yourself and others on the road."

"Hey," she swats at me, but there's no real offense behind her denial. She knows she's a shit driver.

My eyes soften as I look down at the beautiful, sweet, stubborn girl in my arms. "And you were the most beautiful thing I've ever seen. From that first moment...I just couldn't walk away from you."

She cocks her head to the side, "I didn't even know if you really liked me. You were so surly and hardly spoke to me at all. I still don't know much about you or what you do…" she trails off and looks up at me curiously, waiting for an explanation.

I sigh, figuring I owe her this much at least. I if I want to keep her, she has a right to know who she's getting involved with. "You were a distraction. One I didn't need. Nevertheless, one I couldn't let go of."

I look her straight in the eye when I admit my truth to her. "I'm not a good man, Bailey. I don't always play on the right side of the law. I'm king of a criminal empire, though, and I swear to God I'd cut off my right hand before I let something happen to you."

My eyes trail over her pretty little face, drinking in her sweet innocence. "I'm not worthy to breathe the same air as you, let alone touch you." I cup her face, stroking my thumb over her petal-soft cheek. "But I just can't help myself. I'm consumed by you, your fire, your light, your goodness."

I drop my forehead to hers before I make my ragged plea. Me, who's never begged for anything a day in his life. "I *need* you to be mine. I feel like I'll die without you in my life. But you *do* have a choice. As tempted I've been to just take you, I don't want to keep you without your consent. But I do need you to understand the gravity of this. There's no going back for me." I look up at her, trying to impress upon her the seriousness of the situation. "Once I have you, I won't be able to let you go."

Once I make her mine, I'll be completely gone, and I know it. I don't think I'll be physically capable of releasing her, and it's only fair she knows that upfront.

I look down into her eyes that are flickering between brown and green and gold and wait with bated breath as she studies me.

As she holds my frozen heart in her hands.

CHAPTER 8

Bailey

I STARE up into Aidan's green eyes and serious countenance. His mouth is pressed into a firm line, but there's a vulnerability in his eyes I never thought I'd see.

And I still can't believe it's for me, that this darkly alluring criminal wants *me*.

Maybe I should be scared of what all he's admitted to me.

But, strangely, I'm not. I've suspected something dark in him from the beginning.

"How many times have you contemplated kidnapping me?" I ask him with a grin, trying to lighten the mood.

He doesn't smile, though. He's completely somber as he answers, "Every fucking day since I've met you. Too many times to count."

My smile fades at his seriousness, though not because I'm upset. On the contrary, I feel a shiver of pleasure go up my spine that he really wants me that badly. Is something wrong with me that I'm not worried about all this? I don't know, and I really don't care.

In all my life, Aidan has been the only one who's ever acted like he gave a shit about me or what happened to me.

"You're wrong about something," I tell him.

I see his eyebrows shoot up in surprise.

"You're not a bad man," I insist. "Maybe you've done some bad things, but a bad man wouldn't have cared if a stupid girl who can't drive got back on the road and hurt herself or others. A bad man wouldn't have insisted on driving her everywhere just to make sure she got to work and back okay."

Aidan blows out a breath and shakes his head. "It's important that you don't idolize me or ascribe characteristics to me that aren't there, Bailey. It's not that I've done some bad things. I *do* bad things, and I'm sure I'll do more in the future. Especially when it comes to protecting you." His jaw hardens at his last statement as if he's imagining something trying to hurt me.

I can't help it. My heart melts at the thought that he cares about me like that.

"I don't always think everything is so black and white, though," I tell him. "Something tells me you live by a moral code all your own, and I don't think you'd harm innocent people on purpose."

He just stares down at me, his jaw still tight.

I scoot closer to him until my open legs are pressed right against his bulging length. I can almost feel him pulsing against me through his jeans.

He groans, and his hands tighten on my hips. "Bailey, babydoll, I need to know your decision. I can't hold back much longer. I either need to be inside you or get as far as fuck away from you as possible."

I can feel his hands vibrating against my skin, and it gives me a thrill to know that I have him on the edge of his control like that.

My heart starts beating faster within my chest as I lean up and press my lips right against his. "Take me. I'm yours," I move my lips against his as I breathe the words right into his mouth.

That's all it takes to snap whatever thread he's been hanging by. All restraint goes out the window as he crashes his lips down onto mine, kissing me feverishly.

I can't catch my breath. I'm surrounded by him. His arms are around me, pulling me close to his chest as I hear him unzipping his pants.

Then, I feel his velvety, hard flesh slapping against the inside of my thigh. The tip is wet, leaving a trail of fluid in its wake where it slides over my skin. I feel an answering wetness pooling at the apex of my thighs.

"Can't wait, babydoll," he grits out. "Need you now."

He positions himself at my entrance, and I'm suddenly just as frantic as he is. Before he can even push inside me, I'm pushing down.

He groans in surprise, a shudder going through his big shoulders, and I gasp as I feel the tip of him slide inside me, making me feel fuller even than his fingers did.

"Bailey," he says my name, drawing my eyes up to him. "Look at me, baby. You keep your eyes on me as I make you mine."

I feel my pussy clench at his words, and he groans as he pushes further into me.

The pressure is uncomfortable, but I keep staring into his eyes like he commanded me. I watch as his pupils seem to dilate and his nostrils flare as he keeps pushing into me.

I whimper as I feel him stretching me impossibly wide.

"Almost there, baby. I got more to give you. Just hold on."

I bite my lip, and I see his eyes flick down to the motion before they darken, and he suddenly pushes up into me hard.

Something inside me breaks, and I gasp out at the sting, clinging to him on instinct.

He holds my head against him, stroking my damp hair until the stinging subsides, whispering platitudes to me. "Good girl. I'm going to make it all better. It's going to feel so good. Look at how perfect my cock fits inside you. Made for me."

I feel him pulsing within me, and I involuntarily squeeze around him.

"Motherfucker," he curses before he pulls out slightly and pushes back into me.

I let my head fall back and moan at the sensation of him sliding inside me.

"You like that, baby?" he asks right in my ear.

"Uh huh," I moan, and he does it again.

And again. And again. Each time causing tingles to snap throughout me.

He keeps going, getting harder and faster until he's pulling all the way out and thrusting back inside me, impaling me on him.

And it feels so fucking good.

He's panting, his breath coming out in big huffs as his eyes stay glued on me the entire time.

"So fucking beautiful. Mine. Mine. Mine."

His possessive chanting, the way he tightens his jaw, and the way his eyes are half crazed sends waves of pleasure crashing through me.

"Aidan, I—" I don't know what I'm trying to tell him, just to not stop, that I'm on the verge of something.

"Yes, Bailey, yes," he growls out. "Come all over your man's dick. Give it to me, baby."

His encouragement mixed with his hardness pumping in and out of me send me rocketing over the edge.

Pleasure cascades over me, exploding from my core and traveling all the way to the top of my head and the tips of my toes, making me feel weak and floaty all over. It's even more intense than the orgasm he gave me earlier with his tongue, and I'm screaming out his name when it hits me.

"Fuck, baby!" he screams out before I feel him go harder than steel inside me. "Mine!" he bellows as he begins to jerk and pulse inside me, spilling hot liquid into my body. I can feel the warm jets shooting deep within me, and a sense of satiation like nothing I've ever known blankets me.

And when he gathers me into his arms and carries me to my bed, still inside me, laying down and cradling me against his chest like I'm the most precious thing in the world, I can't help thinking that nothing has ever felt more right.

CHAPTER 9

Bailey

I DIDN'T TRULY REALIZE the full extent of what agreeing to be Aidan's would mean.

I didn't know he was going to immediately demand that I come home with him, for instance.

Not that I really have a problem with that. I do want to be with him.

It's just…it's all moving so quickly.

He's like a whirlwind once he gets up and starts moving around. He's packing my meager belongings into the only suitcase I own, telling me that he'll have his "people" come by and pick up anything else I want to take with me.

And I'm just sitting here in bed with the sheet pulled up over my breasts watching him in half amusement, half shock.

Because I know he's dead serious. If there's one thing I've learned about Aidan in the short time I've known him it's that he doesn't joke. Ever. He says what he means and means what he says. If he doesn't have anything to say, he doesn't say anything at all.

He's a man of his word, and when he told me becoming "his" was a serious matter and that there was no coming back from it, he meant it.

Not that I want to come back from it.

I don't.

I just…

I don't know.

He's making my head spin, and I need a moment to think.

"Aidan," I try to break into his whirl of activity.

"What, babydoll?" he doesn't even spare a glance at me as he continues on with his task. My heart flutters at the endearment. I love how he calls me "babydoll," "dollface," "baby."

His phone rings then, and he finally stops moving to answer it.

I don't know what's being said on the other end of the line, but Aidan's mouth presses into a firm line, and he finally says curtly, "I'll be there in ten."

He turns back to me, his expression grim. "I have to take care of something, Bailey. While I'm gone, I want you to stay in your apartment with the door locked. Take a shower, get cleaned up, whatever you want to do. I'll be back for you as soon as I can."

I nod. A shower actually does sound good after getting drenched in the rain and then having my brains fucked out by the insanely hot man who's been driving me around for weeks now.

"Is everything okay?" I ask him.

"It will be, but it's very important that you listen to me. Stay in here, and don't answer the door for anyone. Keep your phone near you and wait for me to call you. I'll be back for you as soon as I can."

I nod at him again, but that's apparently not good enough for him.

He stoops down so he's eye level with me and looks at me seriously. "Do you understand me, Bailey? Don't go anywhere. No sneaking out in flimsy little dresses. This is for your safety."

"Am I in danger?" I ask, suddenly cautious.

He huffs out a breath and runs a hand through his hair. "Not imminently, but I'm not always the most well-liked guy. A lot of people would use you to get to me if they know what you mean to me, and the whole fucking city pretty much knows by now."

My brow furrows in confusion. "They do? How? *I* just found out."

He lets out a bark of laughter. "You were apparently the last one to find out, dollface. A man doesn't threaten the owner of every establishment in the city about a woman's safety without rumors starting to fly."

My eyes widen at his implication. So that's why my life seemed to get so much easier since he came into it. He maneuvered it that way.

Again, I realize that maybe I should be upset at his interference, but I'm not. Instead, I'm grateful. He's the reason my boss finally let up on me. He's the reason why customers have stopped harassing me.

My heart swells with gratitude at the lengths he's gone to to protect me.

He grabs the back of my head and leans in to kiss me before standing and pulling on his leather jacket. His shirt and pants are still damp, but the water has long since slid off his jacket.

"I'll be back soon, babydoll. Lock this door behind me."

I stand with the sheet still wrapped around me and follow him to the door to obey him.

He kisses me again, lingering over my lips, before he finally jerks himself away and walks through the door. I hear his footsteps pause on the other side as he waits to hear the click of the deadbolt sliding into place before he's satisfied enough to take off down the hallway.

As I shower, I can't help wondering what's going on. Is he just being overprotective, or is there some sort of danger?

I take my time getting dressed and actually blow-dry my curls, scrunching them until they're shiny and bouncy, wanting to look pretty for Aidan when he gets back.

I don't know how much time has passed, but it has to have been at least an hour.

I move to the window and look out. My heart leaps up into my chest when I see a black Audi with darkly tinted windows sitting across the street.

There's only one person I know who drives a car like that.

Aidan.

My heart leaps up into my chest, and I run out the door to meet him, completely forgetting his order about waiting for him to call me. Besides, he's here, right? So, everything will be fine. Nothing will ever happen to me with him around. He promised. And I believe him.

I run across the street to the car, a huge smile on my face, ready to throw myself into his arms. I missed him that much in our short time apart.

But when the door opens and a tall figure steps out, my smile quickly fades.

"Well, well, well. What do we have here?" The beefy man with a bald head speculates as he leers down at me. "She ran right to us, boys," he calls back into the car, and I hear chuckles sounding from within it.

My heart plummets within my chest as I realize my error.

He's not Aidan.

CHAPTER 10

Aidan

A TRAP, *a trap, a trap.*

The words beat in my head over and over again in tune to my heart.

It was all a set-up, a trap to get me out here. Fear laces up my spine as I realize the only reason I would have been lured out here.

To get me away from Bailey.

So, they could take her and use her as leverage against me.

I'm driving like a bat out of hell, committing every traffic violation on the books to make it back to her apartment as quickly as possible.

I'm pressing the speed dial button for her number over and over again, but to no avail.

Her phone keeps going straight to voicemail.

And my heart is about to beat out of my damn chest in fear and anger.

I feel panic begin to overtake me as I think of who could have her and what they could be doing to her.

When I finally reach her apartment, I skid to a stop outside the building without even parking properly. I take the stairs two at a time and bust through her door.

My fears are realized when I find her apartment empty.

I let out a roar that even sounds inhuman to my own ears as a deadly cocktail of fear and rage assaults my senses, causing my blood to pump violently through my veins.

I don't know where the fuck she is, but one thing is for motherfucking sure.

I will burn this city to the ground looking for her.

And when I find out who took her, even God won't be able to help them.

I call the head of my security and bark out orders to him, telling him to get me coordinates on Bailey's phone now, praying that it's with her since I don't see it anywhere in the apartment.

I'm coming, babydoll.

Bailey

I feel my phone vibrating against my ass where I have it stuffed into the back pocket of my jeans.

I know it's Aidan calling. He's called over and over again, and by some miracle the men who've taken me haven't heard the vibrations. Perhaps because they're too busy talking loudly, boasting about the reward they're going to get for obtaining the leverage their boss now has on Aidan—namely me.

I don't have a clue where they're taking me, and I desperately wish there was some way I could answer the phone without alerting them.

As it is, I'm sitting in the back seat squished in between two men who are even bigger and burlier than the one who's driving the vehicle.

I haven't been restrained or anything, and I guess it's because what's the point? I'm no match for these men at all. They could demolish me with their pinky fingers. That's how much bigger than me they are.

I'm wracking my brain for anything I can do, but it looks hopeless. All I can do is pray that somehow Aidan will find me.

"What the—" the driver says as he looks in his rearview mirror.

The other men start looking in the sideview mirrors and turning around.

I can't stop myself from turning too.

My heart leaps as hope takes wing in my chest.

Aidan's black Audi is right behind us, gaining quickly. It's flanked by two big, black SUVS that are driving just as fast as Aidan as they tail us.

"Fuck," the driver slams his hand down on the steering wheel in frustration as the Audi speeds up around us.

"Hey, man. I didn't sign up for this. I was just told we were going to get the girl. Not that we were going to be chased down by this crazy motherfucker," the guy sitting in the front passenger seat says.

"Shut up!" The driver screams, his eyes flicking back to me like this is all my fault. "Just shut up and let me think for a minute."

"I say we toss her," one of the guys sitting next to me booms in his deep voice. "Push her out the door and speed off. He'll be too busy checking on her. It'll give us time to get the fuck out of here."

I tense up, not liking the thought of being flung out of a moving vehicle but wondering if it's the only chance I have of making it out of this. If I don't die, that is.

Before the guys can ever reach a decision, I'm

suddenly thrust forward as the driver curses and slams on the brakes.

We go spinning until we skid to a stop, and when I look up and out of the front window, I see why.

Aidan's Audi swerved sideways, effectively cutting us off. The two SUVs quickly pull up on either side of us, flanking us in.

Suddenly, the back door is being swung open, and Aidan roughly pulls the guy blocking me from him from the vehicle, squarely landing a punch in his face before flinging him to the ground, knocked out cold. He reaches back inside and gathers me in his arms, pulling me free.

I cling to him, the tears suddenly coming in a torrent, as the guy on the other side of me is yanked out of the other side of the door by one of the guys from one of the black SUVs that were working with Aidan.

"Sshh," he tries to comfort me where I'm shaking uncontrollably in his arms. "I've got you, Bailey. I've got you."

"Take care of this," he barks to his guys.

"You got it boss," one of them says.

Aidan doesn't say another word to them. I'm clinging to him with everything in me, my arms and legs wrapped tightly around him as I sob into his neck, my whole body shaking with the adrenaline of what just happened.

"I'm so sorry," I babble. "I thought it was you. I thought it was you in the Audi."

He shushes me again, running a hand up and down my back. "I've got you baby. I've got you. And I'm never going to let you go."

I look up at him then, needing to see his green eyes. I see how harried he looks, the wildness that's still in his eyes. "I love you, Aidan."

His eyes flare with a new light, and he cups the side of my face with one hand. "I love you too, Bailey. So motherfucking much. God, you don't even know." His voice breaks before he sucks in a shaky breath and goes on, "You'll never truly understand the depth of my feelings for you. I'd do anything to make sure you're safe."

I calm slightly at his words as I take in deep breaths, the fact that he saved me finally settling over me and slowing my racing heart.

"Even go all road rage and go on a high-speed chase for me," I hiccup up at him, tears still glistening in my eyes.

He cracks a grin and gives a relieved chuckle. "I even borrowed a page from your book and cut the fuckers off."

I laugh, startled that my dark, serious Aidan actually made a joke.

"Sorry again about that," I grin back up at him.

He shakes his head. "I'm not. Otherwise, I might not have ever met you."

"And where would I be without you to drive me around?" I point out.

His grin widens. "Exactly, and you better believe I'm the only one who's going to be driving you for the rest of our lives."

That dark lock of hair falls over his forehead as he leans down to kiss me, that electric current that pulses between us charging our lips and sealing our hearts together.

"Let me drive you home," he whispers against my lips.

"Always," I tell him. Anywhere I go now, I want it to be with him.

Always with him.

EPILOGUE

One Year Later

Aidan

"JUST A COUPLE MORE STEPS," I breathe into my wife's ear as I guide her with my hands over her eyes. I'm taking her to where her surprise is waiting.

My cock twitches in my pants at the shiver that runs through her body at my breath fanning her ear. I'm always half hard when I'm around her, and I inhale a deep breath, trying to get ahold of myself, knowing that one kiss, one thought of her creamy skin will be enough to get me going.

"Aidan," she laughs as she says my name, and I

can't stop the smile that overtakes my face. I've never smiled so much as I have this past year of knowing her.

"Okay," I tell her, removing my hands from her eyes.

I'm looking down at her beautiful face, watching every expression flit across it. Surprise, wonder, happiness.

I drink it all in, loving how I can read everything she's thinking right there in her eyes.

I had her uncle's convertible properly restored with a new paint job and a top that actually works.

"It's beautiful," she breathes. She walks over and runs her fingers along the top of the door.

"Want to take it for a test drive?" I ask her.

She looks up at me in surprise, a delicate brow raised. "I thought you said I'd never get behind the wheel of this car again."

I've been teaching her to drive a stick shift, but that doesn't mean I want her on the road just yet—if ever. I love driving her everywhere, and she loves it too, I know.

Besides, I still run my empire, though I've definitely pulled back on many of the more dangerous tasks and delegated those to my most trusted advisors.

I can't be putting Bailey at risk. I need to be here for her, to watch over her and protect her. Support her in anything she wants to do.

And she wants to do a lot of things. I'll never get over how curious she is. She's tried her hand at painting, writing, singing. She seems to be good at everything she does, but she's still finding herself, figuring out what she wants to do the most.

And I'm there for her every step of the way, making sure that I can make whatever she wants happen.

I want to give her the world.

I smirk at her, "That's not the type of test drive I was talking about."

Her face colors as she catches the innuendo in my statement. Then, she walks over to me, the little green dress she's wearing swishing gently around her thighs and bringing out all the green and gold flecks in her eyes.

She trails her fingertips up my chest before she circles my neck loosely with her arms.

I place my hands on her waist, feeling the silky strands of her curls tickling the backs of my hands.

"I don't know if I can handle an engine this size," she tells me innocently, chewing on her bottom lip.

My cock swells until it's pushing against the zipper of my jeans.

She knows I can't take it when she worries her lip like that.

"I'll be there to help you drive it," I reassure her. I grind my cock against her through her dress as I begin to trail my hands up the backs of her thighs to her tight little ass.

I hiss in a breath when my hands trail over bare skin. Moisture begins leaking out of the head of my cock, and I can't stop myself from rocking it roughly against her, humping her bare flesh through my jeans.

"Fuck, you're not wearing any panties, babydoll." I slip a finger into her, testing her wetness.

"Is it because that pussy's been just waiting for my cock to breed it?"

I've been dying to get her pregnant, plant my seed inside her, and see her grow round with my child. A little piece of her and me.

A family.

She moans at my words, but I don't even give her a chance to answer me.

I open the driver's side door and sit down in the seat before deftly unzipping my pants. My cock bobs free just as I pull her onto my lap, impaling her on me in one hard thrust.

She's so wet I slide right in, though she's still so tight I damn near see stars when I'm finally engulfed in her hot heat.

"Oh god," she cries out.

"Nuh-uh," I chide her. "Only me, baby. You say my name when it's my cock splitting you open."

"Aidan," she corrects herself as I show her no mercy, pumping up into her savagely.

My balls are so tight it's almost painful. I can feel her wetness dripping down onto them.

"Want me to put a baby up inside you?" I pant at her. I'm so close. I'm going to blow at any minute.

I reach down between us and pass my thumb over her clit. That's all it takes for her to detonate.

Her hand flails behind her, looking for purchase, and lands on the horn. The long wail of the horn sounds out as she falls apart on me, her pussy sucking and milking at me until I can't take it anymore and finally release into her. I push my dick as far up into her as I can get it while I dump my load into her womb and hold myself there as I jerk and pulse inside her.

I let my head fall forward to rest on her chest, listening to her heart thumping away as I wrap my arms around her back, still seated inside her.

There's nowhere on earth I'd rather be that right here, balls deep in her, holding her tenderly.

"I have a surprise for you too," she tells me with a mischievous smile.

I pull back just enough to arch an eyebrow up at her, wondering what she has up her sleeve.

She leans down to kiss me gently before she whispers, "You've already put a baby inside me. I'm pregnant."

I jerk back to look into her eyes fully, my chest instantly expanding with hope.

"When? How long have you known?" I force myself to relax my hold on her arms, not wanting to hurt her in my excitement.

"I took a pregnancy test this morning," she says, "but I'm two weeks late and have suspected for a little while now."

My heart explodes with joy, and I hug her tightly to me.

I finally truly have everything.

And it's all thanks to her. I thank God every day for the day she wrecked my heart and sped into my life like a little bat out of hell.

THE END

Connect with Emma!

Visit Emma's website to get a FREE book you can't get anywhere else: www.authoremmabray.com.

9 798821 569382 7